The Song of Six Birds

For my grandchildren,
a reminder of the beauty of birdsong – R.D.

To Margaret, who loves birds – L.G.

The Song
of Six Birds

written by Rene Deetlefs
with illustrations by Lyn Gilbert

A

Andersen Press
London

Lindiwe lay on her grass mat, sleepily aware
of the music of morning as it stole into her ears:
cattle lowed, buckets tinkled and goats bleated.
    Lindiwe yawned, then blinked her eyes.
Next to her, on the smooth, cool floor, lay a flute,
an African flute, just like the ones in the wayside store!

"Mama," she whispered, "is this flute for me?"
"Indeed, Lindiwe," smiled her mother, as she played
with the baby. "It is for you, child who loves music."

Up jumped Lindiwe.
"Mama!" she cried. "A flute is *full* of music!
Just listen!"

Putting her lips to the flute, she drew a mighty breath
and blew. What a shattering noise! The dozing dog
started up and howled. The chickens squawked
and the baby screamed with fright.

Lindiwe peered into the dark tunnel of her flute.
No sign of music there!
"What's wrong with this flute?" Lindiwe wondered.
"I must find music for it."

So off she went –
past two old mamas weaving grass mats,
all the way to the river in search of music for her flute.

"Mahem!" called a crowned crane, preening himself in the morning sunlight.

"Crane," begged Lindiwe, "share your trumpet call with me! This flute needs music."

"Mahem!" trumpeted the royal bird.
The echo of his call flew into Lindiwe's flute.
"Thank you!" she shouted, jumping from stone
to stone as she crossed the river.

A boy was herding goats on the other side.
"Tock-tocki-tock," a hornbill called from a rock.
"Hornbill," said Lindiwe, "you see my flute?
It is new and cannot yet sing like you.
Share with me a 'tocki-tock'."

The hornbill obliged, and into Lindiwe's flute
fell the bright, round sound.
"Thank you, Hornbill," she cried.

Along a dusty path, a woman was hanging blankets on a bush to air. Unseen, a bird sang, "Doo, doo-doo-doo." Quiet as a mouse, Lindiwe listened to the soft, falling notes.

"Don't hide from me, Rainbird," she whispered.
"This flute needs a song from you."
But the rainbird would not open its beak.

So Lindiwe waited, and waited . . .
At last, from among the leaves, the rainbird appeared.
Holding out her flute, Lindiwe quickly caught a
"Doo-doo-doo".
"Thank you, shy Rainbird," she softly said.

Then, suddenly, Lindiwe shrieked.
A hornet's sting burned her arm.

Off she ran to the village medicine man who was
quietly gathering herbs nearby.
"Look at my arm!" sobbed Lindiwe. "Look at my flute!
I don't want the sound of sobs inside it!"

The wise old man smiled, laying a cool herb leaf
on her throbbing arm.
  "But a flute should sometimes sob," he said.
"Ask that hoopoe."

Lindiwe turned and saw the hoopoe, searching
the ground for insects. Raising and lowering his crest
he cried, "Hoop, hoop!"
Lindiwe wiped away her tears.
 "Hoopoe, please share your song with me!"

So, "Hoop, hoop!" he called again.
Lindiwe laughed. The mellow song
was safely in her flute.

On the edge of the village, Lindiwe stood aside for an old man riding his bicycle. A jar, heavy with honey, was balanced on his carrier. Following him was a Paradise Fly-catcher.

"Wheewheeo-wit-wit!"
The tiny ripple of sound settled on the tip of her flute.

Now the sun hung low and Lindiwe's shadow
was long. Just before the sun set, a wood owl called:
"Whoo-hu, whoo-hu-hu!"

Lindiwe caught the sound in her flute.
She peered into it and a smile spread slowly
over her face. The song of six birds filled it.

It was time to hurry home
and hurry home she did,
followed by the six birds.
They all made music while she ran.

Together their joyous sounds
carried through the village,
calling everyone to join in the fun.

Humming and swaying to the music,
the two old mamas left their looms. Then the boy
and his goats came capering along. Singing like a bird
ran the woman with the blankets. Prancing and chanting
came the medicine man, and dancing like he used to
long ago, came the old man with the bicycle.

Lindiwe's mother, hearing all the jolly sounds,
smiled proudly.

"Here, my child of music," she said, "I have made my special stew so all can join in a feast."

Now eating, now singing, now dancing, the happy party went on long into the night. And the air was filled with the music of Lindiwe's flute – and the song of six birds.

First published in Great Britain in 1999 by Andersen Press Ltd., 20 Vauxhall Bridge Road, London SW1V 2SA. Published in Australia by Random House Australia Pty., 20 Alfred Street, Milsons Point, Sydney, NSW 2061. All rights reserved. Colour separated in Italy by Fotoriproduzione Grafiche, Verona. Printed and bound in Italy by Grafiche AZ, Verona.

10   9   8   7   6   5   4   3   2   1

British Library Cataloguing in Publication Data available.

ISBN 0 86264 852 1

This book has been printed on acid-free paper